Ten Red Apples

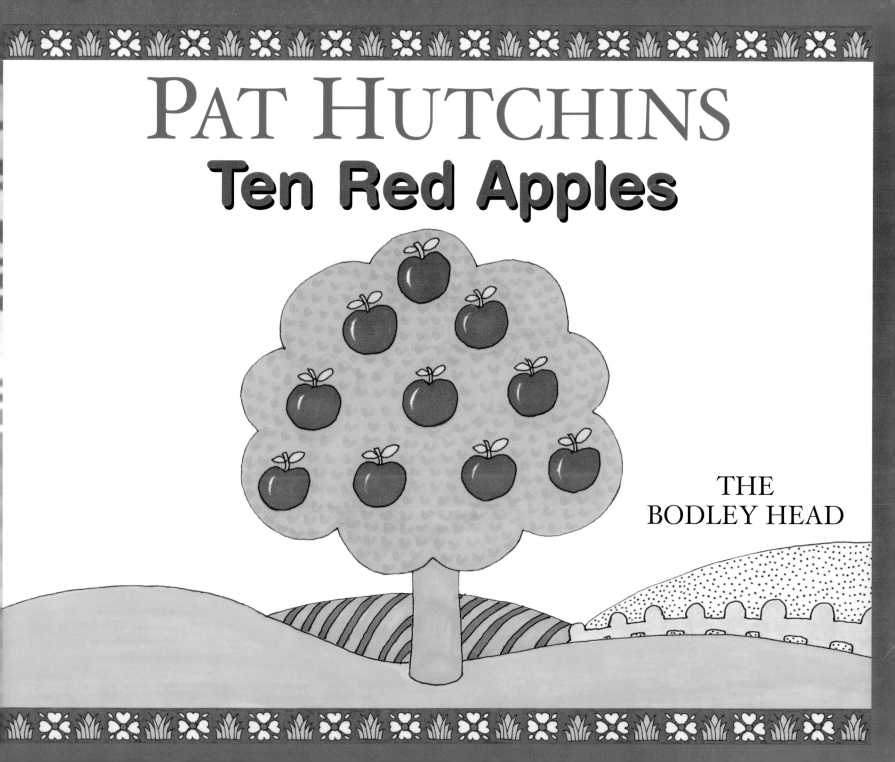

PAT HUTCHINS
Ten Red Apples

THE
BODLEY HEAD

1 3 5 7 9 10 8 6 4 2

Copyright © Pat Hutchins 2000

Pat Hutchins has asserted her right under the
Copyright, Designs and Patents Act, 1988,
to be identified as the author and illustrator of this work

First published in the United Kingdom 2001
by The Bodley Head Children's Books
Random House, 20 Vauxhall Bridge Road, London SW1V 2SA

First published by Greenwillow Books, New York 2000

Random House Australia (Pty) Limited
20 Alfred Street, Milsons Point, Sydney
New South Wales 2061, Australia

Random House New Zealand Limited
18 Poland Road, Glenfield
Auckland 10, New Zealand

Random House South Africa (Pty) Limited
Endulini, 5A Jubilee Road,
Parktown 2193, South Africa

THE RANDOM HOUSE GROUP Limited Reg. No. 954009
www.randomhouse.co.uk

A CIP catalogue record for this book
is available from the British Library

ISBN 0 370 32693 8

Printed and bound in Singapore

For my great-nephew, Owen.

10

Ten red apples hanging on the tree.
Yippee, fiddle-dee-fee!

Horse came and ate one,
chomp, chomp, chomp.
Neigh, neigh, fiddle-dee-fee.
"Horse!" cried the farmer.
"Save some for me!"

9 🍎🍎🍎🍎🍎🍎🍎🍎🍎

Nine red apples hanging on the tree.
Yippee, fiddle-dee-fee!

Cow came and ate one,
munch, munch, munch.
Moo, moo, fiddle-dee-fee.
"Cow!" cried the farmer.
"Save some for me!"

8

Eight red apples hanging on the tree.
Yippee, fiddle-dee-fee!

Donkey came and ate one,
gobble, gobble, gobble.
Hee-haw, fiddle-dee-fee.
"Donkey!" cried the farmer.
"Save some for me!"

7 Seven red apples hanging on the tree.
Yippee, fiddle-dee-fee!

Goat came and ate one,
gulp, gulp, gulp.
Maa, maa, fiddle-dee-fee.
"Goat!" cried the farmer.
"Save some for me!"

6 🍎🍎🍎🍎🍎🍎

Six red apples hanging on the tree.
Yippee, fiddle-dee-fee!

Pig came and ate one,
snort, snort, snort.
Oink, oink, fiddle-dee-fee.
"Pig!" cried the farmer.
"Save some for me!"

5

Five red apples hanging on the tree.
Yippee, fiddle-dee-fee!

Sheep came and ate one,
nibble, nibble, nibble.
Baa, baa, fiddle-dee-fee.
"Sheep!" cried the farmer.
"Save some for me!"

4 🍎🍎🍎🍎

Four red apples hanging on the tree.
Yippee, fiddle-dee-fee!

Goose came and ate one,
crunch, crunch, crunch.
Hiss, hiss, fiddle-dee-fee.
"Goose!" cried the farmer.
"Save some for me!"

3

Three red apples hanging on the tree.
Yippee, fiddle-dee-fee!

Duck came and ate one,
pick, pick, pick.
Quack, quack, fiddle-dee-fee.
"Duck!" cried the farmer.
"Save some for me!"

2

Two red apples hanging on the tree.
Yippee, fiddle-dee-fee!

Hen came and ate one,
peck, peck, peck.
Cluck, cluck, fiddle-dee-fee.
"Hen!" cried the farmer.
"Save one for me!"

1 🍎

One red apple hanging on the tree.
Yippee, fiddle-dee-fee!

"Good," said the farmer.
"You saved one for me!"
Yippee, fiddle-dee-fee!

O

No red apples hanging on the tree.
My, my, fiddle-dee-fee.
No red apples to bake in a pie.
Fie, fie, fiddle-dee-fee!

"Look!" cried the farmer.
"Another apple tree!"

More red apples hanging on a tree.
Yippee, fiddle-dee-fee!
"Good!" cried the farmer's wife.
"You saved them for me!"

Yippee, fiddle-dee-fee!

Since the publication of *Rosie's Walk* in 1968, reviewers on both sides of the Atlantic have been loud in their praise of Pat Hutchins's work. Pat Hutchins, her husband, Laurence, and their sons, Morgan and Sam, live in London, England.